GOLDILOCKS AND
THE THREE BEARS

Goldilocks
and the

THREE BEARS

Retold and illustrated by Jan Brett

PAPERSTAR

The Putnam & Grosset Group

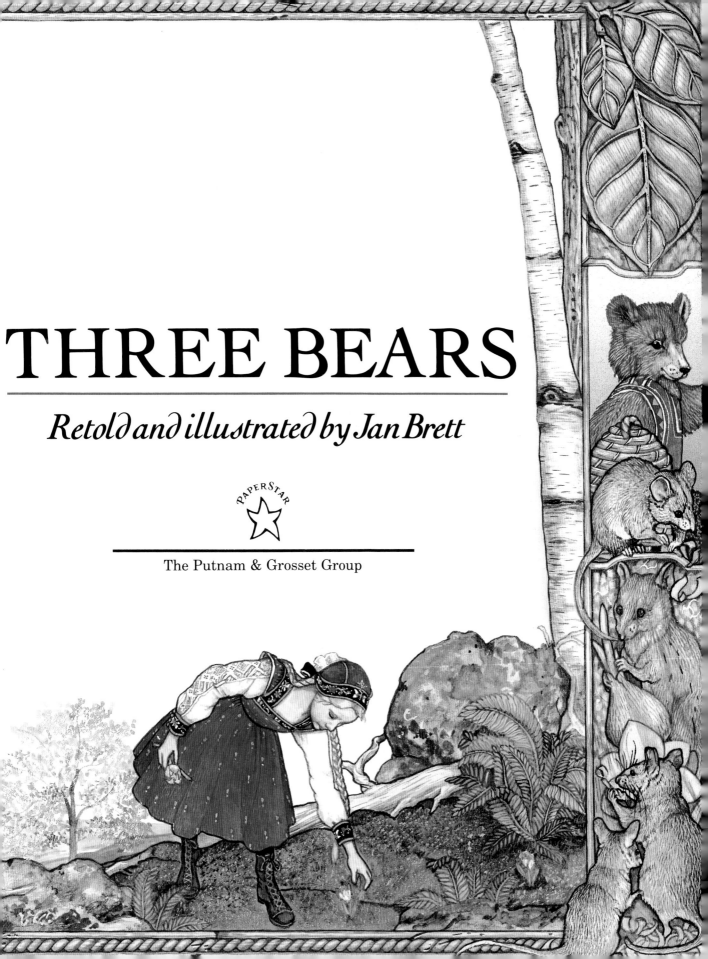

The text for this edition has been adapted from
The Green Fairy Book, edited by Andrew Lang,
published by Dover Publications, Inc., New York.

A PaperStar Book, published in 1996 by The Putnam & Grosset
345 Hudson Street, New York, NY 10014.
PaperStar is a registered trademark of The Putnam Berkley Group, Inc.
The PaperStar logo is a trademark of The Putnam Berkley Group, Inc.
Originally published in 1987 by Dodd, Mead & Company, New York.
Published simultaneously in Canada. Manufactured in China

Library of Congress Cataloging-in-Publication Data
Brett, Jan. Goldilocks and the three bears/retold and illustrated by Jan Brett.
p. cm. Summary: Lost in the woods, a tired and hungry girl finds the
house of the three bears where she helps herself to food and goes to sleep.
[1. Folklore. 2. Bear—Folklore.] I. Title.
PZ8.1.B755Go 1989 398.2'1—dc19 [E] 89-3778 CIP AC
ISBN 0-698-11358-6
Special Markets ISBN 978-0-399-25491-8 Not for resale
3 5 7 9 10 8 6 4 2

This Imagination Library edition is published by Penguin Group (USA), a Pearson
company, exclusively for Dolly Parton's Imagination Library, a not-for-profit
program designed to inspire a love of reading and learning, sponsored in part by The
Dollywood Foundation. Penguin's trade editions of this work are available wherever
books are sold.

For Betty, Sallie, and Joe,
and for Miriam

Once upon a time there were three bears who lived together
in a house of their own in a wood.

One of them was a little, small, wee bear, and one was a
middle-sized bear, and the other was a great, huge bear.

They each had a bowl for their porridge—a little bowl for the little, small, wee bear, a middle-sized bowl for the middle-sized bear, and a great, huge bowl for the great, huge bear.

And they each had a chair to sit in—a little chair for the little, small, wee bear, a middle-sized chair for the middle-sized bear, and a great, huge chair for the great, huge bear. And they each had a bed to sleep in—a little bed for the little, small, wee bear, a middle-sized bed for the middle-sized bear, and a great, huge bed for the great, huge bear.

One day, after they had made their porridge for breakfast,
and poured it into their porridge bowls, they walked out into
the woods while the porridge was cooling.

And while they were walking, a little girl named Goldilocks came to their house. First, she looked in at the window, then she peeped in at the keyhole, and seeing no one was at home, she lifted the latch.

The door opened before her, and in she went.

How pleased Goldilocks was when she saw the steaming porridge on the table. The sweet smell of the porridge with roasted nuts, honey, and berries filled the room. It was so tempting that Goldilocks set about helping herself.

First she tasted the porridge of the great, huge bear, but it was too hot. Then she tasted the porridge of the middle-sized bear, but it was too cold. And then she tried the porridge of the little, small, wee bear, and it was neither too hot nor too cold, it was just right. She liked it so much that she ate it all up.

Then Goldilocks sat down in the chair of the great, huge bear, but it was too hard for her. Then she sat down in the chair of the middle-sized bear, but it was too soft for her.

And then she sat down in the chair of the little, small, wee bear, and this chair was neither too hard nor too soft, but just right. So Goldilocks seated herself in it, and there she sat until the bottom of the chair gave way, and down she came—plump! —upon the floor.

Then Goldilocks went upstairs to the bedroom in which the three bears slept.

First she lay down upon the bed of the great, huge bear, but that was too high at the head for her. Next she lay down upon the bed of the middle-sized bear, but that was too high at the foot for her. Then she lay down upon the bed of the little, small, wee bear, and that was neither too high at the head nor foot, but just right. So she covered herself up comfortably and fell fast asleep.

By this time the three bears thought their porridge would be cool enough to eat, so they returned home for breakfast. Now Goldilocks had left the spoon of the great, huge bear standing in his porridge.

"SOMEBODY HAS BEEN AT MY PORRIDGE!" said the great, huge bear, in his great, rough, gruff voice.

And when the middle-sized bear looked at hers, she saw that the spoon was standing in it too.

"Somebody has been at my porridge!" said the middle-sized bear, in her middle voice.

Then the little, small, wee bear looked at his bowl, and the spoon was in the porridge bowl, but the porridge was all gone.

"Somebody has been at my porridge, and has eaten it all up!" said the little, small, wee bear, in his little, small, wee voice.

Upon this, the three bears, seeing that someone had entered their house, and eaten up little, small, wee bear's breakfast, began to look about them. Now Goldilocks had not put the hard cushion straight when she rose from the chair of the great, huge bear.

"SOMEBODY HAS BEEN SITTING IN MY CHAIR!" said the great, huge bear, in his great, rough, gruff voice.

And Goldilocks had crumpled the soft cushion of the middle-sized bear.

"Somebody has been sitting in my chair!" said the middle-sized bear, in her middle voice.

And you know what Goldilocks had done to the third chair.

"Somebody has been sitting in my chair, and has sat the bottom right out of it!" said the little, small, wee bear, in his little, small, wee voice.

Then the bears thought it necessary that they should make a further search, so they went upstairs to their bedroom. Now Goldilocks had pulled the pillow of the great, huge bear out of its place.

"SOMEBODY HAS BEEN LYING IN MY BED!" said the great, huge bear, in his great, rough, gruff voice.

And Goldilocks had pulled the cover of the middle-sized bear out of its place.

"Somebody has been lying in my bed!" said the middle-sized bear, in her middle voice.

And then the little, small, wee bear came to look at his bed. There was Goldilocks—sleeping peacefully, her long shiny braids spread across his pillow. Little, small, wee bear just stared at her, for a moment, and didn't say anything.

But then he cried, "Somebody has been lying in my bed—
and here she is!"

Goldilocks had heard in her sleep the great, rough, gruff voice of the great, huge bear, and the middle voice of the middle-sized bear, but it was only as if she had heard someone speaking in a dream. But when she heard the little, small, wee voice of the little, small, wee bear, it was so sharp, and so shrill, and so like her own, that it awakened her at once.

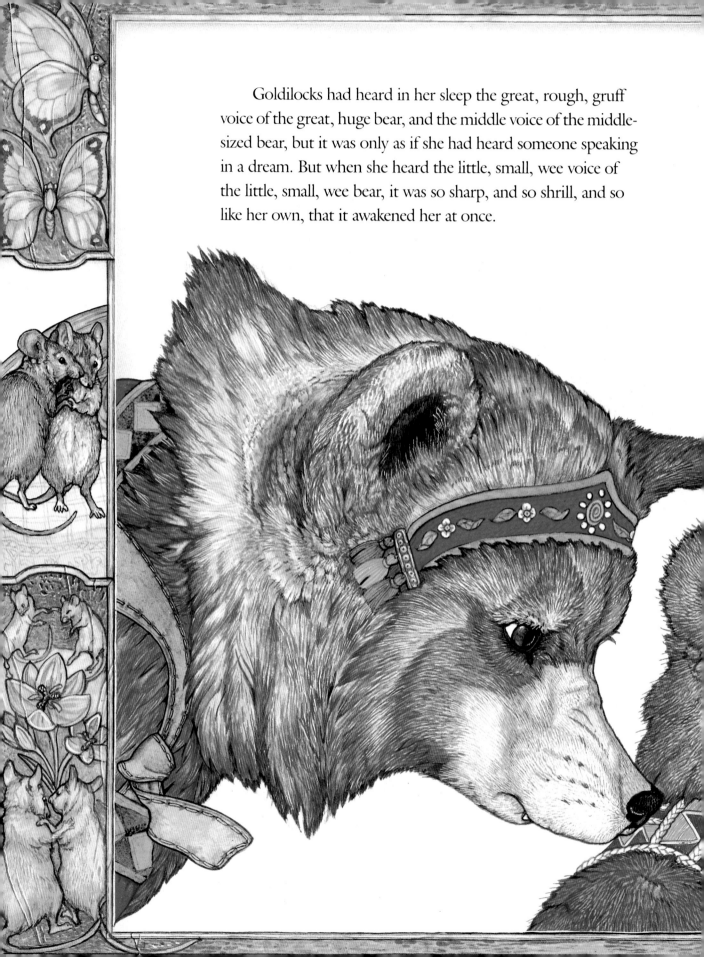

Up she started; and when she saw the three bears on one side of the bed, she tumbled herself off the other, and ran to the window.

Out Goldilocks jumped, and ran away as fast as she could run—not looking behind her until she was very far away.

And what happened to Goldilocks afterwards, no one can tell. But the three bears never saw anything more of her.